anythink

I0604909

NO LONGER PROPERTY OF
ANYTHINK LIBRARIES/
RANGEVIEW LIBRARY DISTRICT

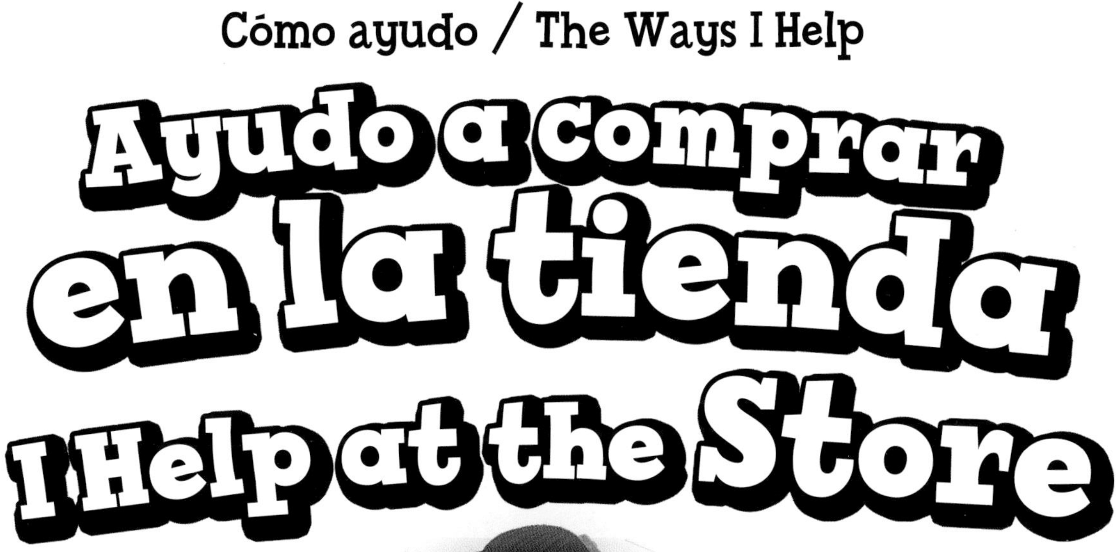

Sadie Woods

traducido por / translated by Alberto Jiménez

ilustrado por / illustrated by
Aurora Aguilera

New York

Published in 2018 by The Rosen Publishing Group, Inc.
29 East 21st Street, New York, NY 10010

Copyright © 2018 by The Rosen Publishing Group, Inc.

All rights reserved. No part of this book may be reproduced in any form without permission in writing from the publisher, except by a reviewer.

First Edition

Translator: Alberto Jiménez
Editorial Director, Spanish: Nathalie Beullens-Maoui
Editor, English: Theresa Morlock
Book Design: Raúl Rodriguez
Illustrator: Aurora Aguilera

Cataloging-in-Publication Data

Names: Woods, Sadie.
Title: I help at the store = Ayudo a comprar en la tienda / Sadie Woods.
Description: New York : PowerKids Press, 2018. | Series: The ways I help = Cómo Ayudo | In English and Spanish | Includes index.
Identifiers: ISBN 9781508157168 (library bound)
Subjects: LCSH: Shopping–Juvenile fiction. | Helping behavior–Juvenile fiction.
Classification: LCC PZ7.W663 Ihe 2018 | DDC [E]–dc23

Manufactured in the United States of America

CPSIA Compliance Information: Batch #BS17PK: For further information contact Rosen Publishing, New York, New York at 1-800-237-9932

Contenido

Contents

Hoy vamos a hacer la compra.

Today we are going food shopping.

Ayudo a mi mamá a escribir la lista
de lo que necesitamos.

I help my mom write a list of what we need.

Le recuerdo que hay que llevar bolsas para traer la comida a casa. Las bolsas reutilizables son mejores que las de plástico.

I remind her to bring bags to carry the food home. Reusable bags are better than plastic bags.

En el supermercado agarramos un carrito. Mi hermano se sienta en él.

At the store we pick out a shopping cart. My brother sits in the cart.

Yo me encargo de llevar la lista

de la compra y las bolsas.

It's my job to carry the shopping list and the bags.

Primero escogemos la fruta. ¡Yo elijo tres manzanas crujientes y tres peras jugosas! Después las tacho de nuestra lista.

First we pick out fruit. I choose three crunchy apples and three juicy pears! Then I check them off our list.

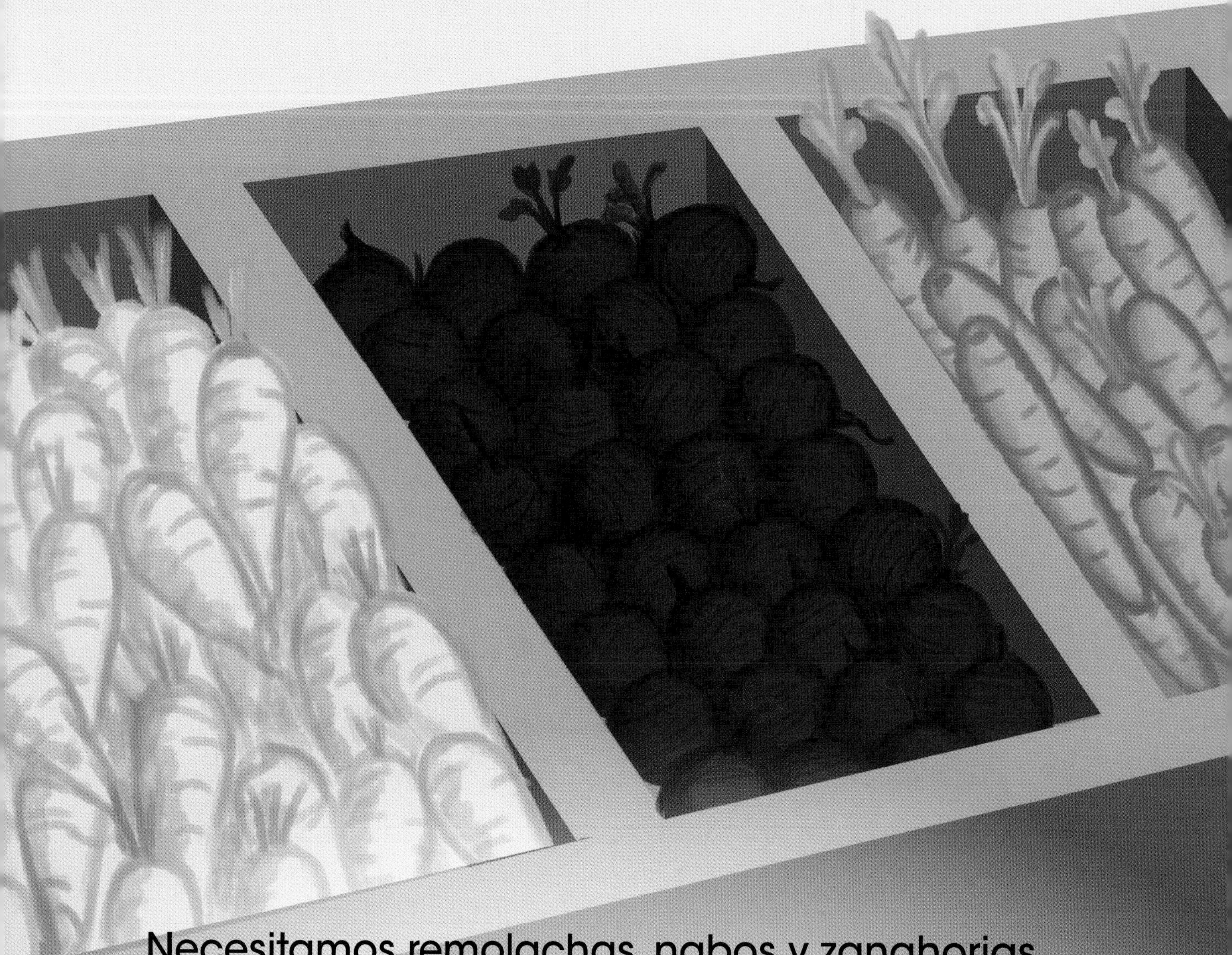

Necesitamos remolachas, nabos y zanahorias.
Compramos frutas y verduras maduras.

We need beets, turnips, and carrots.
We buy fruits and vegetables that are ripe.

Ayudo a mamá a pesar las frutas y
las verduras en una báscula.

I help mom weigh the fruits and
vegetables on a scale.

La báscula imprime etiquetas con los precios.

The scale prints price tags.

La próxima cosa en nuestra lista es el arroz.
Escojo una bolsa grande de arroz.

Rice is next on our list. I pick up a big bag of rice.

Ya solo nos queda una cosa en la lista.

¡Necesitamos huevos!

We just have one more thing on our list.

We need eggs!

Los cargo con cuidado
para que no se rompan.

I carry the eggs carefully
so they don't break.

Llevamos el carrito al cajero.

We take our cart up to the cashier.

Coloco los artículos en la cinta transportadora.

I place each item on the conveyer belt.

¡Estoy deseando ver qué ricos platos prepararemos con nuestra compra!

I can't wait to see what tasty meals we will make with the food we bought!

ET

Palabras que debes aprender
Words to Know

(el) cajero
cashier

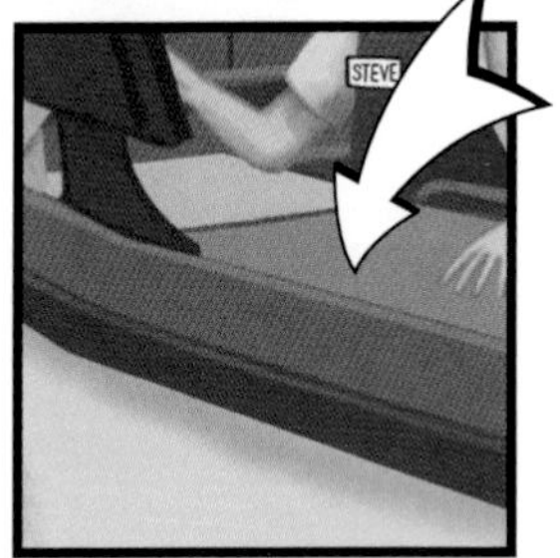

(la) cinta transportadora
conveyor belt

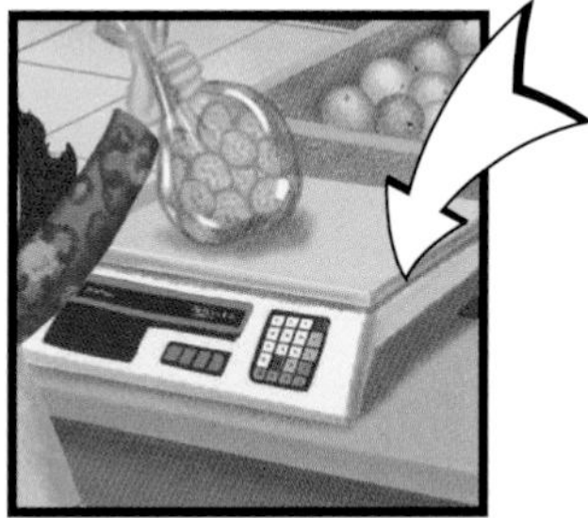

(la) báscula
scale

Índice / Index